WALT DISNEY'S
GRANDPA BUNNY

Told by Jane Werner

Illustrated by the Walt Disney Studio

Adapted by Dick Kelsey and Bill Justice
from the motion picture *Funny Little Bunnies*

A Golden Book • New York

Copyright © 1951, 2007 Disney Enterprises, Inc. All rights reserved. Published in the
United States by Golden Books, an imprint of Random House Children's Books, a
division of Random House, Inc., New York, and in Cananda by Random House of
Canada Limited, Toronto, in conjunction with Disney Enterprises, Inc. GOLDEN BOOKS,
A GOLDEN BOOK, A LITTLE GOLDEN BOOK, the G colophon, and the distinctive gold spine
are registered trademarks of Random House, Inc.
www.goldenbooks.com www.randomhouse.com/kids
Educators and librarians, for a variety of teaching tools, visit us at
www.randomhouse.com/teachers
Library of Congress Control Number: 2005937035   ISBN: 978-0-375-83930-6
Printed in the United States of America   First Random House Edition 2007
10 9 8 7 6 5

Deep in the woods, where the briar bushes grow, lies Bunnyville, a busy little bunny rabbit town. And in the very center of that busy little town stands a cottage— a neat twig cottage with a neat brown roof—which is known to all as the very own home of Great Grandpa Bunny Bunny.

Great Grandpa Bunny Bunny, as every bunny knows, was the ancestral founder of the town, which is a very fine thing to be.

He liked to tell the young bunnies who always gathered around how he and Mrs. Bunny Bunny, when they were very young, had found that very briar patch and built themselves that very same little twig house.

It was a happy life they lived there, deep in the
woods, bringing up their bunny family in that little
house of twigs.

And of course Daddy Bunny Bunny, as he was called
then, was busy at his job, decorating Easter eggs.

As the children grew up, they helped paint Easter eggs. And soon they were all grown up, with families of their own. And they built a ring of houses all around their parents' home.

By and by they had a town there, and they called it Bunnyville.

By that time, Grandpa Bunny Bunny had lots of help painting Easter eggs—so much that he began to look for other jobs to do.

He taught some of the young folks to paint flowers in the woods. They tried out new shades of green on mosses and ferns.

They made those woods so beautiful that everyone who went walking there marveled at the colors.

"The soil must be especially rich," they said, "or the rainfall especially wet."

And the bunnies would hear them and silently laugh. For they knew it was all their Grandpa Bunny Bunny's doing.

Years went by. Now there were even more families in
Bunnyville. And Grandpa Bunny Bunny had come to be
Great Grandpa Bunny Bunny. For that is how things go. He
still supervised all the Easter egg painting, and the work on
the flowers every spring.

But he had so much help that between times he looked
around for other jobs to do. He taught some of the
bunnies to paint the autumn leaves—purple for the gum
trees, yellow for the elms, patterns in scarlet for the sugar
maple trees. Through the woods they scampered with
their brushes and their pails.

And everyone who went walking there would say, "Never has there been such color in these woods. The nights must have been especially frosty hereabouts."

And the bunnies would hear them and silently laugh. For they knew that it was all their Great Grandpa Bunny Bunny's plan.

And so it went, as the seasons rolled around. There were constantly more bunnies in that busy Bunnyville.

And Great Grandpa was busy finding jobs for them to do.

He taught them in winter to paint shadows on the snow . . .

. . . and pictures in frost on wintry windowpanes, and to polish up the diamond lights on glittering icicles.

And between times he told stories to each new crop of bunny young, around the cozy fire in his neat little twig home. The bunny children loved him and his funny bunny tales. And they loved the new and different things he found for them to do.

But at last it did seem as if he'd thought of everything!
He had crews of bunnies trained to paint the first tiny buds
of spring.

He had teams who waited beside cocoons to touch up
the wings of new butterflies.

Some specialized in beetles, some in creeping,
crawling things.

They had painted up that whole wild wood till it
sparkled and it gleamed.

And now, the bunnies wondered, what would he think of next? Well, Great Grandpa began to stay at home a lot more, and he thought and thought and thought.

And at last he told a secret to that season's bunny boys and girls.

"Children," Great Grandpa Bunny Bunny said, "I am going to go away. And I'll tell you what my next job will be, if you'll promise not to say."

So the bunny children promised. And Great Grandpa Bunny Bunny went away. The older bunnies missed him, and often they looked sad. But the bunny children only smiled and looked extremely wise. For they knew a secret they had promised not to tell.

Then one day, a windy storm rained down on Bunnyville. Everyone scampered speedily home and stayed cozy and dry indoors.

After a while, the rain slowed to single dripping drops.
Then every front door opened, and out the bunny
children ran.

"Oh, it's true!" the bunnies shouted. And they did a
bunny dance. "Great Grandpa's been at work again.
Come see what he has done!"

And everyone walking out that day looked up in pleased surprise.

"Have you ever," they cried, "simply *ever* seen a sunset so gorgeously bright?"

The little bunnies heard them and they quietly chuckled. For they knew it was all Great Grandpa Bunny Bunny's plan.